NED
WHO AM I REALLY?

WRITTEN AND ILLUSTRATED BY
KRISTIN GATTENS AND NICOLE REGAN

EAST 26TH
PUBLISHING

NED: Who Am I Really?

Libary of Congress Cataloging-in-Publication data is available
ISBN: 978-1-7348856-3-7

10 9 8 7 6 5 4 3 2 1
First printing edition 2020

East 26th Publishing
Houston, TX

www.east26thpublishing.com

TO MOM AND DAD—
FOR ALL THE BOOKS YOU READ TO US,
THIS ONE IS FOR YOU.
LOVE, KRISTIN AND NICOLE

It was a regular day, in a regular year.
Ned was out in the garden when a thought flew past his ear.

"You are Ned," said the thought. Ned heard the thought loud and clear.
What a strange thing to think! What an odd thing to hear.
"Of course, I am Ned," Ned heard himself say.
But the thought did not leave him. The thought did not go away.

Then the thought made a question, as thoughts often do,
"But who are you, REALLY...and what makes you, YOU?"
What a fantastical question for such a regular day!
Ned searched for an answer, but what could he say?

HA! HA! HA!
HEE! HEE! HEE!

"Well, I'm just a kid. And I'm seven years old.
I'm a boy...I have glasses...and my hair's kind of gold.
I like skateboards and reading. I'm a brother and a son.
I know lots of dinosaurs—I can name every one.
I have a pet frog and his name is Pickles.
He's a very good listener and he loves belly tickles."

"Does that make me, ME? Does that make me Ned?
Did I answer your question with all the things that I said?"
Ned took a big breath and sat still for the thought.
He wasn't quite sure if he'd hear it or not.

And then, just like magic, Ned felt the thought near...
not sure it was real until it jumped in his ear.
"These things are all lovely; they are close to your heart.
Not quite the true answer, but a fabulous start!"

"You see, these things will change, they won't stay the same.
So, you're MORE than these things. You're even more than your name!"
Ned was confused. "MORE what? MORE how?
And what's going to change? Please tell me right now!"

"You are more than you see. You are more than you know.
Ned, most things will change. And we need change to grow!
You'll change and you'll grow, but you'll always be YOU!
No matter what things you like. No matter what things you do."

"You're not just your body. You're not just your mind!
There's a magic inside you and it's one of a kind.
This is not super-obvious. It's no easy task.
But lucky for you, you know just who to ask."

And then, just like that, the thought disappeared.
Ned whispered softly, "Oh boy, that was weird!"
It was all a bit puzzling...Ned's chat with the thought.
And he wasn't too sure if he should tell someone or not.
What if they laughed? Or said things that were rude?
Ned felt rather nervous with his curious mood.

And then Ned remembered the thought said he was lucky.
So, he felt a little more grateful and a little less yucky.
Ned knew just what to do! Ask Nanny next door!
He knew she would help him; that's what nannies are for.

Ned called through the window, "I'll be with Nanny next door!"
His mom smiled and waved, "Just be back by four!"
Ned hopped, skipped and jumped through the garden and up each stair.
He gave the door a loud knock and hoped Nanny was there.

Nanny flung the door open with delight in her eyes.
"Ned! My darling boy! What a lovely surprise!"
"I have something to ask you, Nanny. It might sound a bit silly.
But what makes me, ME? And who am I, REALLY?"

"What MARVELOUS questions!" Nanny squealed with glee.
"Big questions like these will need big cups of tea!
Come on in straight away! I'll make us some chai.
Have a seat in the lounge and I'll warm up some pie."

Ned flopped on the sofa and saw something dash.
It was Nanny's cat, Ninja—a big fluffy flash.
"I wish Ninja liked me," Ned said with a sigh.
"Don't mind him," Nanny snickered, "He's always been shy.
That's why he's called Ninja—he's tricky and stealth!
We can't try to change him—it's not good for his health!"

Nanny brought in the goodies and set them down on the table.
"Now! Tell Nanny what's happened...and I'll help if I'm able."
Ned took a big bite of the warm apple pie
and chewed terrifically slowly because he felt terrifically shy.

"I heard something strange, Nanny. Perhaps I just made it up?"
Ned looked down at the table and picked up his cup.
"It sounded like a thought, but I could talk to it too.
I know that sounds crazy! Has it happened to you?"
Nanny smiled with her lips and she smiled with her eyes.
She chose her words kindly because kindness is wise.

"A strange occurrence indeed. But I believe you, don't worry!
The line between real and imagined is often quite blurry.
Tell me more about this thought and all that was said.
We'll have a good chat until it makes sense in your head."

So, Ned told Nanny everything. He told her the lot.
What the thought said to him and what he said to the thought.
He told her of changing and growing and what stays the same;
Of the magic inside him and that he's more than his name.
When he was finished, he looked up with a smile.
And his heart felt a freedom it hadn't felt in a while.

Nanny took a deep breath and gave Ned's hand a squeeze.
"I'm so thankful for you and for moments like these.
What you just shared is special. It was an honor to hear!
An amazing experience; not something to fear."

"What I'm about to explain is what I know to be true.
But you must only believe what feels right for you.
There are things in this world that aren't well understood.
We can't pretend to know everything. That won't do anyone good.
But since you've come here and asked, my opinion is this:
The thought helped you notice what can be easily missed."

NED AGE 75

NED AGE 50

PICKLES AGE ???

"Some people think we are just what we do,
or just how we look, but that's not totally true.
For instance, you said your hair's kind of gold.
Perhaps true today, but what about when you're old?
Your hair might be white, it might be a bit grey,
but you'll still be you because there's no other way."

"The thought made you wonder about what doesn't change.
And the answer, my dear, is wonderfully strange!
It's true, what you heard. You have a magic inside.
In fact, we all have it. It's not something to hide."

"Some call it the spirit. Some call it the divine.
It has different names and that's perfectly fine."
It's the light of the universe—a connection to God.
So many ways to describe it...which is fantastic, not odd.
Some call it your soul or your innermost being.
It's the constant awareness that's always knowing and seeing."

"It feels like meaning and purpose. It feels like stillness and love.
It inspires our becoming. It creates dreams to dream of.
To explain something big with words that are small
is a challenge indeed. Does this make sense at all?"
Ned took a moment to ponder. It was a lot to take in.
He had so many questions, but where to begin?

"I'm not totally sure that I get what you mean.
How is there a part of me that can't even be seen?"
"Just because we can't SEE it, doesn't mean it's not there.
For example, did you notice Ninja snuck under your chair?!
He's always around us, he just loves to hide.
It doesn't mean he's not there. You'd spot him if you tried."

POP!

"There are ways to know something we can't see, touch or smell.
We must open our minds. We must open them well.
It takes study and practice, but the idea is this:
You can use your awareness to know what other senses miss.
If you listen to your breath and sit very still,
you can quiet your mind – it's a valuable skill!"

"With patience and practice you can learn to feel
the light of your being and the YOU that is real."
"What does it feel like, Nanny? Does it feel nice?
Will you help me practice? I might need some advice!"

"I'm here for you always," Nanny gave Ned's hand a kiss,
"And the light of your being feels like infinite bliss!"

"Have you ever heard music that made your hair give you tickles?
Or felt a big wave of love when you snuggle with Pickles?"

"Perhaps you watched a film that sent tears down your face?
Or you showed someone kindness and felt your heart fill with grace?"

"These things touch your spirit–they make your real self sing.
Your soul echoes joy in your body, which is a wonderful thing!"
Ned grinned a big grin, his heart relaxed and content.
He'd felt ALL of these feelings, so he knew just what Nanny meant.
"Thanks for your help, Nanny! But I wonder about the thought...
Where did it come from? Was it real or was it not?"

Nanny took a moment to answer. She looked up and away.
Ninja perked up an ear to hear what she would say.

"I can't tell you for certain, but one thing is hard to ignore.
The thought told you of things you did not know before.
Which gives me a clue; the thought wasn't just in your mind.
Our soul has infinite wisdom–its words are loving and kind.
Don't worry too much about what's real or not.
It felt real to you and that counts for a lot."

Ned sipped his last sips of his big cup of tea
and glanced at the clock; it was 3:53!
"I have to go, Nanny! Mom said be back by four.
I wish I could stay longer and talk even more."

3:53!

"You'd best get going! Give my love to your mom."
Ned gave Nanny a hug while Ninja crept away with a crumb.
Ned felt very grateful as he walked out the door.
He knew who he was really...just a little bit more.

As Ned stepped into the garden,
a bluebird danced past his head...

and Ned swore he heard the thought whisper,
"Welcome home. You are Ned."

ABOUT
the
AUTHORS

Kristin and Nicole are long-time friends, who met over 15 years ago while teaching English to children in South Korea. They have travelled the world together many times over and maintain a friendship that is rooted in fun, inspiration, encouragement, joy, and adventure.

Kristin Gattens is originally from Vancouver, Canada and now lives in a seaside village on the South Coast of England. Kristin has an established counseling practice, Inspired Soulutions, where she works as a spiritual counselor and empowerment coach. She has a master's degree in counseling psychology and spent the formative years of her career working in child psychiatry and mental health services.
Kristin's heart beats a little quicker when she is marveling at everyday magic, belly laughing with friends, exploring new places, and helping other people enjoy being themselves.

Nicole Regan's most recent move has been from Vancouver, Canada to the jungles of Costa Rica. She is a nurse with an extensive background in palliative care and has supported patients and families in various hospitals and a children's hospice. Nicole teaches yoga and meditation online and spends her free time creating art, attempting waves, and concocting fabulous new adventures with friends and family.

NED is the creative manifestation of two friends following their hearts, learning to have an authentic and intentional presence within the world, and using their gifts in service.

Made in the USA
Columbia, SC
15 May 2021